This is

's

book

For Ronnie —J.M.G.

For Matthew, Ben, James, Thomas,
and for John for staying up late —A.H.

Text copyright © 1993 Jeanne M. Gravois
Illustrations copyright © 1993 Alison Hill

First published in Great Britain in 1993 by **ABC**

This edition first published in 1994 by softbacks,
an imprint of **ABC**, All Books for Children,
a division of The All Children's Company Ltd.
33 Museum Street, London WC1A 1LD

Printed and bound in Hong Kong

British Library Cataloguing in Publication Data
Gravois, Jeanne M.
Quickly, Quigley. - New ed
I. Title II. Hill, Alison
823

ISBN 1-85704-047-3

Quickly, Quigley

Written by Jeanne M. Gravois
Illustrated by Alison Hill

Quigley was small.
And Quigley was slow.
In the morning he got ready for school.
Whenever Mum came in to check,
he had his boots on the wrong feet.

"Quickly, Quigley," said Quigley's mum.
"And don't forget your hat and boots."

Quigley was small.
And Quigley was slow.
When he went to school he drew pictures.
Some days he lost his red crayon,
some days he lost his green crayon.

"Quickly, Quigley," said Quigley's teacher.
"Come join the class."

Quigley was small.
And Quigley was slow.

When the bell rang it was
time to play.
The little penguins ran outside;
he was always the last one.

"Quickly, Quigley," said Quigley's friends.
"Catch up."

Quigley was small.
And Quigley was slow.

When dinner was ready, Mum called him.
By the time he sat down,
Mum and Dad had
finished.

"Quickly, Quigley," said Quigley's parents.
"Finish eating so you can play."

Quigley was small.
And Quigley was slow.
When it was bedtime,
there were toys all over the room,
and he was still playing.

"Quickly, Quigley," said Quigley's dad.
"Clean up, then I'll read to you."

Quigley was small.
And Quigley was slow.
One spring day his brother was born.
Things changed at home,
and he was busier than ever.

"Quickly, Quigley! Fetch the baby's shoes!"
"Quickly, Quigley! Get a blanket for your brother!"
"Quickly, Quigley!"

One day Quigley took his brother
to meet his friends.
"Quickly, Quigley!" they called.
Quigley ran to catch up,
when he heard a small voice cry,
"Quigley . . .

. . . slow down!"